Text copyright © 2009 by Lauren Thompson · Illustrations copyright © 2009 by Jon J Muth
All rights reserved. Published by Scholastic Press, an imprint of Scholastic Inc., *Publishers since 1920*.
SCHOLASTIC, SCHOLASTIC PRESS, and associated logos are trademarks and/or registered trademarks of Scholastic Inc.

No part of this publication may be reproduced, stored in a retrieval system, or transmitted in any form or by any
means, electronic, mechanical, photocopying, recording, or otherwise, without written permission of the publisher.
For information regarding permission, write to Scholastic Inc., Attention: Permissions Department, 557 Broadway,
New York, NY 10012.   ISBN-13: 978-0-439-77497-0 · ISBN-10: 0-439-77497-7 · LC number: 2008043308

LIBRARY OF CONGRESS CATALOGING-IN-PUBLICATION DATA AVAILABLE
10 9 8 7 6 5 4 3 2 1   09 10 11 12 13   Printed in Singapore 46

For Robert and Owen – L. T.
Uncle Michael, Santa surely,
time and again. – J. M.

First edition, September 2009
The art was created using watercolors and pastels.
The text was set in 20-point Kennerly.
Book design by David Saylor and Charles Kreloff

THE
CHRISTMAS
MAGIC

BY LAUREN THOMPSON · PICTURES BY JON J MUTH

SCHOLASTIC PRESS · NEW YORK

*F*ar, far north, where the reindeer are, there is
a snug little house with a bright red door. And
in that house lives Santa Claus.

Every year, just when the nights are
longest and the stars shine brightest,
Santa feels a tingling in his whiskers.

Then he knows that the
Christmas magic will soon be here.

First, Santa gathers the reindeer
from the sparkling fields of snow.

"Come along home now," he calls to them.
"The magic will be here soon."

In the cozy barn, Santa brushes the
burrs from the reindeer's shaggy coats
and treats them to parsnips and berries.

Then he swings open a creaky old door
that has been closed since Christmas last.
Behind that door waits the big red sleigh.

Santa rubs its rounded sides,
and the sleigh softly gleams.

Then Santa lifts the harness from its hook and polishes the bells till they jingle together brightly.

The reindeer raise their heads when they hear the music of the bells: *Is the magic here?*

"No, not yet," Santa tells them. "It's not here yet."

Inside his snug little house, Santa oils
his old black boots with care. He darns the
holes in his thickest wool socks.

He combs his curly white beard
and gives his moustache a trim.

Then Santa climbs
the creaking staircase
to the room at the top
of the house.

This is the room where all the toys are kept, toys of every kind. And here, too, Santa keeps a thickly bound book, and the names of all the children are written in this book.

Santa runs his fingertip down
the crinkling pages. One by one, he
reads each child's name aloud and
smiles.

For Santa loves them all, and
he knows what each child at heart
wants most.

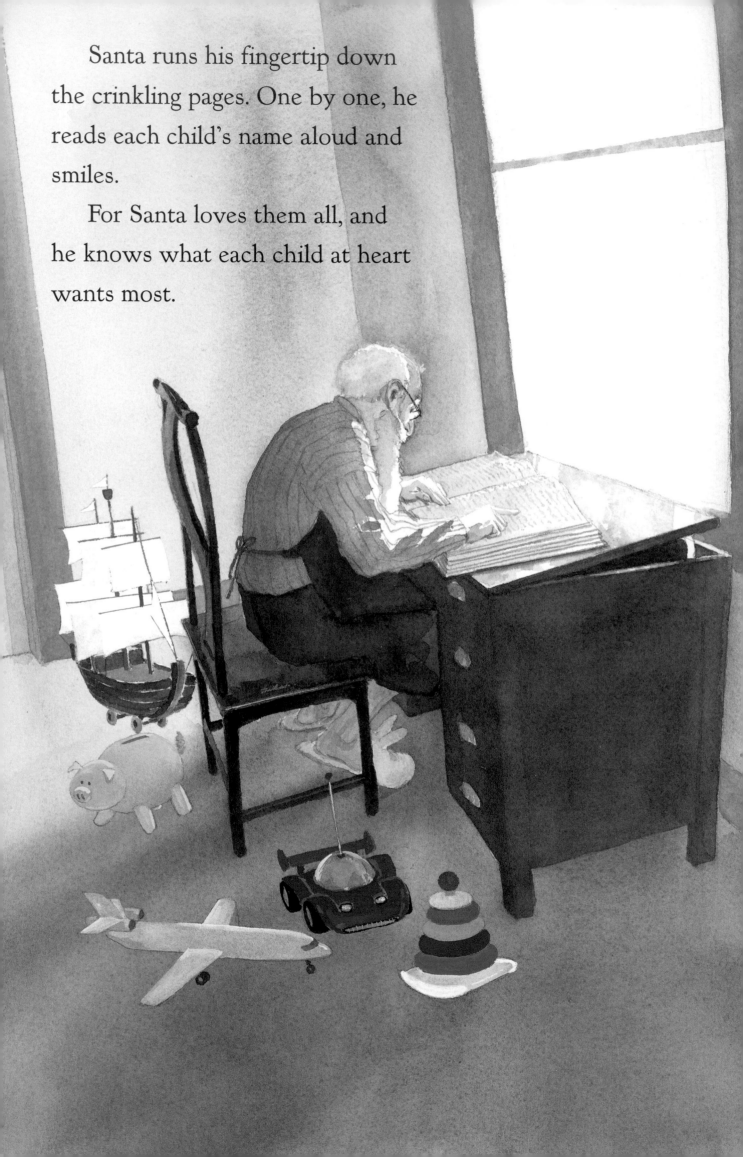

Then he chooses a certain toy and
tucks it into his creased leather sack.
And always the magic draws closer.

When every gift has been chosen
and the pack is nearly overflowing,
Santa closes the bundle up tight.

All is ready.

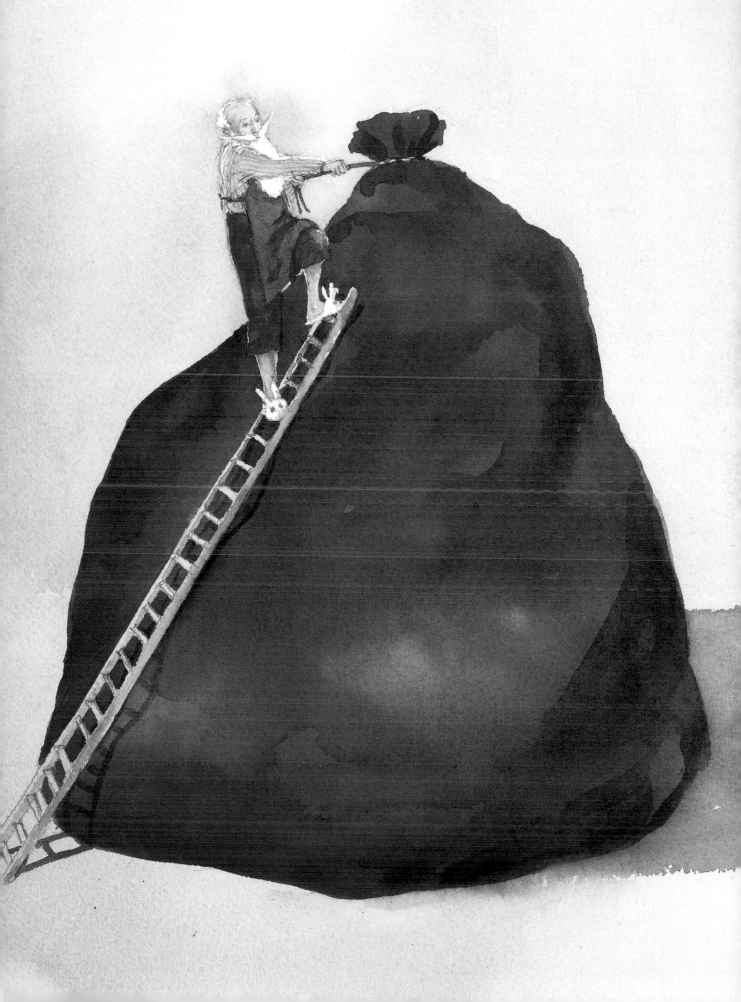

Then this deep winter's night, the stars begin to shine more brightly than ever.
They fill the dark night with their flaming light.

Now in their harness, the reindeer paw
at the snow. They know the magic is near,
very near.

Santa knows, too. He gazes up at the
brilliant, numberless stars, and he thinks of
all the children and how he loves them so.

Suddenly, a warm tingling spreads
from his whiskers to his soles.

And around him, the night begins to thrum with magic, the kind of magic that makes reindeer fly.

With a shake of the reins, Santa calls to his team:
"Hie! Let's be off!" The reindeer pull hard at the harness,
and the bells begin to jingle.

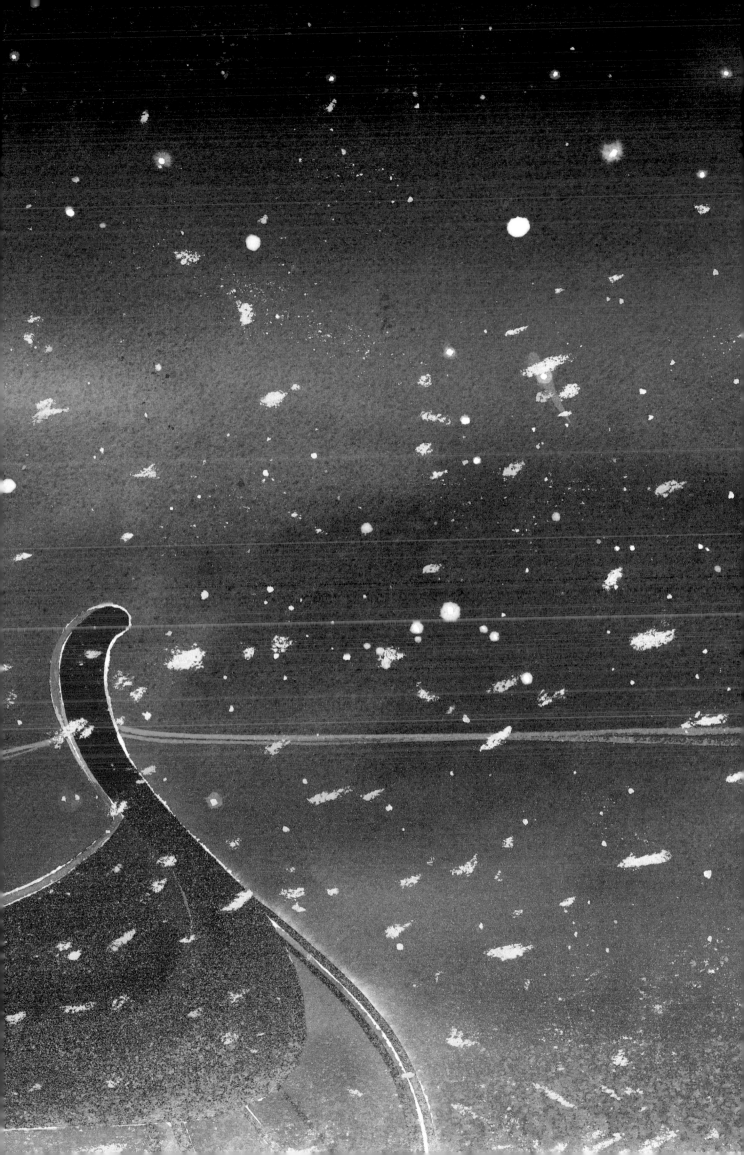

Soon the sleigh is speeding across the snow, and all at once Santa and the reindeer are climbing steeply through the air. Santa sees his little house glowing far below. The stars light the way above.

The Christmas magic is here at last. It has
come at last, as it always has, and always will.